Other Kipper Books

Picture Books

Kipper
Kipper and Roly
Kipper's Birthday
Kipper's Christmas Eve
Kipper's Monster
Kipper's Snowy Day
Kipper's Toybox
Where, Oh Where, Is Kipper's Bear?

Little Kippers

Arnold	Rocket
Butterfly	Sandcastle
Hissss!	Skates
Honk!	Splosh!
Meow!	Swing!
Picnic	Thing!

Board Books

Kipper's Book of Colors
Kipper's Book of Numbers
Kipper's Book of Opposites
Kipper's Book of Weather

Touch and Feel Books

Kipper and the Egg
Kipper's Kite
Kipper's Sticky Paws
Kipper's Surprise

Sticker Stories

Kipper Has a Party
Kipper in the Snow

Lift the Flap

Kipper's Lost Ball
Kipper's Rainy Day
Kipper's Sunny Day
Kipper's Tree House

We won't
need you
till much,
much later.

For information about permission to reproduce selections from this book,
please write Permissions, Houghton Mifflin Harcourt Publishing Company,
215 Park Avenue South, NY, NY 10003.

www.hmhco.com

First published in Great Britain in 2000 by Hodder Children's Books
First Red Wagon Books edition 2001

Red Wagon Books is a trademark of Harcourt, Inc., registered
in the United States of America and other jurisdictions.

The Library of Congress has cataloged the hardcover edition as follows:
Inkpen, Mick.
Kipper's A to Z: an alphabet adventure/written and illustrated by Mick Inkpen.
p.   cm.
Summary: Kipper the dog and his friend Arnold work through the
alphabet by collecting animals and other things for each letter.
[1. Dogs—Fiction. 2. Animals—Fiction. 3. Alphabet.] I. Title.
PZ7.I564Kik   2000
[E]—dc21   00-8853
ISBN 0-15-202594-4
ISBN 0-15-205441-3 pb

SCP 10 9
4500493074

Mick Inkpen

Kipper's

A to Z

An Alphabet Adventure

Red Wagon Books

Harcourt, Inc.

Orlando   Austin   New York   San Diego   Toronto   London

This is Kipper's little
friend, Arnold.
Arnold has found
an ant.

A a is for ant.

And Arnold.

Bb is for box

and buzzzzzzzzzzzzzzzzzzzzzzzzzzzzzzzzzzzzzzzzzzzzzzzzzz

They put the ant
in the box,
and followed
the bumblebee.

ZZZZZZZZZZZZZZZZZZZZZZZZZZZ

It flew away.

"Let's find something beginning with C," said Kipper.

But the caterpillar had already found them!

Cc is for Crawly caterpillar.

D d is for duck.

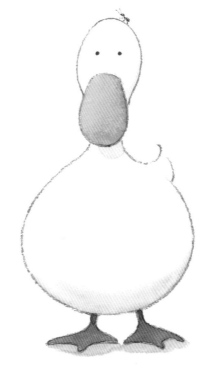

"Duck!" said Arnold.
The duck was too big
to fit into Arnold's box.
And so was the...

enormous

E e is for
empty.

elephant!

Where is the ant?

Ee
is for
elephant.

The frog would have
fit in Arnold's box,
but Kipper couldn't
catch it.
It was too fast!

Ff is for frog.

Arnold was still
wondering where the ant
had gone, when a little
green grasshopper jumped
straight into his box.
"Good!" said Kipper.

G g is for
grasshopper.

Hh is for hill and happy.

They skipped all the way to the top

of Big Hill, and down the other side.

Arnold found another
interesting insect.
He opened his box
and put the interesting
insect inside.

I i is for insect.

They went home for
a glass of juice.
Arnold helped himself
to some jam, too.

J j is for juice.

And a bit of jam, too.

Kipper couldn't think of anything beginning with K. Can you think of anything?

Kk is for...

L was easy.
Outside there were
lots of ladybugs.
Lots and lots.
Arnold put one
in his box.

L l is for
lots of ladybugs.

Arnold found some little muddy mountains.

He was so busy playing that he didn't even notice the mole.

M m is for mole

and mud.

"Is it my turn now?"
said the zebra.
"No, not now!"
said Kipper.
"You don't
begin with N."

Nn is for

No, not now!

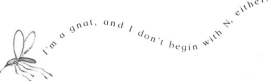

Arnold climbed On the swing.

O o is for on...

And then he fell **O**ff again.

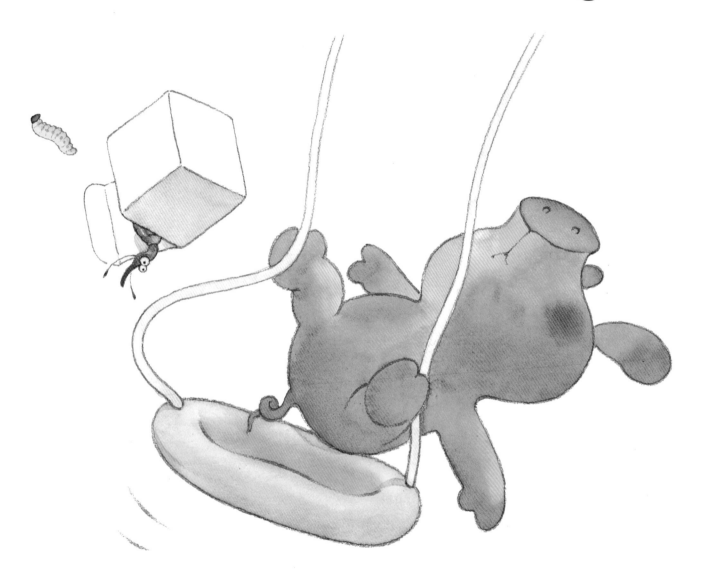

and **off.** And oo is for oops!

Arnold was upset.
He sat up puffing and
panting and a little pink.
So Kipper took him to
his favorite place.
The pond.

P p is for puff, pant, pink,

and pond.

Quack!
Quack!
Quack!

Quack!

Is that Arnold's ant?

Quack!

Quack!

Quack!

Q q is for quiet!

And quack, of course.

It started to rain.

Rr is for rainbow.

They splashed home
through the puddles.

S s is for

Splish!
Splosh!
Splash!

And six squishy slugs.

At home Kipper got out his toys.

T t is for toys.

"I know what begins with U!" said Kipper. "Umbrella!"

They played under the umbrella, while the rain poured down outside.

Uu is for Under the umbrella.

"V is very, very hard," said Kipper. "Do you think we could find a volcano?" Arnold shook his head. So they made a picture of one instead.

V v is for volcano!

The rain stopped.
They looked out the
window to see what
they could see for W.

W w is for

Not long now!

wiggly worm.

But what begins with X?
Kipper thought
and thought
and thought.
He thought of box,
which ends with X, and
he thought of socks,
which doesn't.

"I know!" he said
suddenly. Kipper picked
up the interesting insect.

Xx is for Xugglybug!

"It must be my turn
by now!" said the zebra.
"Is it my turn?
Is it?
Is it?"

Yy is for
Yes!

So the zebra stood
in the middle of the page,
and we all said,

Z z is for Zebra!

zzzzZZZ

And for Arnold's little Zoo, too.